40687-0 · U.S. $2.99
CAN. $3.50

Something Queer at the Birthday Party

by
Elizabeth Levy

illustrated by
Mordicai Gerstein

ISBN 0-440-40687-0

9 780440 406877

50299>

OTHER YOUNG YEARLING BOOKS YOU WILL ENJOY:

YEARLING BOOKS/YOUNG YEARLINGS/YEARLING CLASSICS are designed especially to entertain and enlighten young people. Patricia Reilly Giff, consultant to this series, received her bachelor's degree from Marymount College and a master's degree in history from St. John's University. She holds a Professional Diploma in Reading and a Doctorate of Humane Letters from Hofstra University. She was a teacher and reading consultant for many years, and is the author of numerous books for young readers.

For a complete listing of all Yearling titles,
write to Dell Readers Service,
P.O. Box 1045, South Holland, IL 60473.

Something Queer at the BIRTHDAY PARTY

by
Elizabeth Levy
illustrated by
Mordicai Gerstein

A Young Yearling Book

To George, SURPRISE! Happy Birthday!

E.L.

To Risa with Love

M.G.

Published by
Dell Publishing
a division of
Bantam Doubleday Dell Publishing Group, Inc.
1540 Broadway
New York, New York 10036

ISBN: 0-440-40687-0

Reprinted by arrangement with Delacorte Press

Printed in the United States of America

May 1993

10 9 8 7 6 5 4 3

WES

Jill had figured out the most fiendish plan for surprising Gwen on her birthday. She giggled every time she thought about it.

She invited some of Gwen's friends to help her plan the party. "If we pull this off, it's going to be the surprise of the century," said Sam as he stuffed the last invitation into the envelope. Fletcher licked it.

They walked to the mailbox to mail the invitations. Suddenly Fletcher's tail began to wag. His ears perked up.

"Oh, no, it's Gwen," cried Jill. "Quick, grab the envelopes. If she sees me with them, she'll suspect something. You know she loves mysteries."

Jill shoved the invitations at Willie. He put them behind his back and passed them to Bonnie, who passed them to Sam, who palmed them to Julia, who passed them to Sarah, who put them in the mailbox.

RSVP MEANS, RÉPONDEZ S'IL VOUS PLAIT, WHICH IS FRENCH FOR, ANSWER IF YOU PLEASE.

A week passed. Then just a few days before the party, Jill went over her list. "Mom, a lot of people haven't RSVPed," she complained.

"Well, sometimes people forget," said Jill's mother. "Why don't you call?"

Jill phoned the first name on her list.

"I didn't get an invitation," said Tanya. "I heard about the party, and I was hurt." Jill told Tanya she was definitely invited. It turned out that five invitations had gotten lost in the mail.

TANYA'S VOICE

Jill was determined that the pièce de résistance at the party would be Fletcher jumping out of a cake. She found a big round cardboard box and covered it with frosting. But Fletcher thought jumping was for fleas, not for him. Then Jill found the perfect solution. She tied a piece of salami to a balloon and floated it over the cake. Fletcher loved salami. For salami, even Fletcher would jump.

SALAMI

BIG ROUND CARDBOARD HATBOX

CHOCOLATE FROSTING

When the big day arrived, Jill called Gwen on the phone. "Happy birthday," said Jill in a sad voice.

"What's wrong?" asked Gwen.

"I don't want to ruin your birthday," said Jill. "But we've had a disaster. We've been robbed."

"Oh, no," said Gwen. "I'll be right over."

"What was stolen?" Gwen asked, rushing into Jill's living room.

Jill pointed to the blank wall over the sofa. "The painting of Fletcher and me," she said.

"That's terrible," said Gwen. "That's my favorite painting in the world."

"We called the police," said Jill's mother.
"They couldn't find any clues. That picture meant
so much to me."

Jill's mother winked at Jill. Jill rolled her eyes.
She hoped Gwen didn't see her mother's wink.

Gwen tapped her braces. She always tapped
her braces whenever something queer was going on.

MAGNIFIED VIEW OF HAIR

Gwen looked under the sofa. Fletcher licked her nose. "A clue!" exclaimed Gwen. "A long blond hair! You and your mom are redheads."

"Cherchez la blonde," said Jill's mother.

"Right," said Gwen. "What does it mean?"

"Look for the blonde," said Jill's mom. "They always say that in mysteries."

"This blonde left a string of clues," said Gwen. Gwen followed the blond hairs down the hall toward Jill's room.

SMALL CHIP OF PAINT

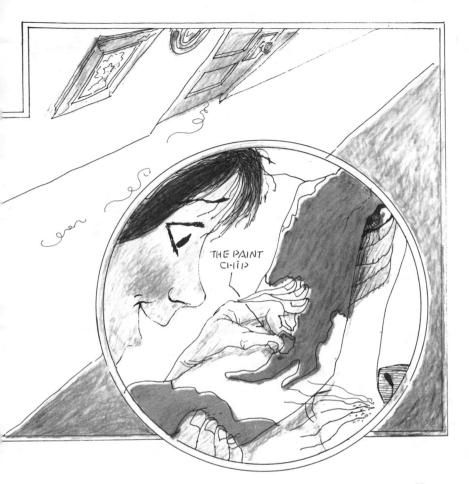

Gwen pointed to a small paint-chip on the wall. She held it up to Fletcher's fur. The color matched exactly the spot on Fletcher's ear that looked like Italy. "I don't know how the police could have missed all these clues," she said.

"They need a great detective to help them," said Jill.

Gwen nodded. "I'm glad you called me."

Gwen tiptoed up to the door of Jill's room. She put her ear to it. "We know that the thief is a blonde and walked this way," said Gwen. "Maybe she hid the painting in your room. Maybe you surprised her in the act."

"That's impossible," said Jill. "Nobody could hide anything in my room, it's such a mess. Don't go in there, Gwen."

"A messy room makes the perfect hiding place," said Gwen. "I've got to go in there."

Gwen opened the door. The room was pitch-dark.

"We need some light," said Gwen. She felt for the light switch on the wall.

"SURPRISE! SURPRISE!" yelled all Gwen's
friends.

Sam and Willie jumped up from under the
bed. Risa, Ona, and Isa leaped out of the closet.
Julia and Sarah hopped down from the desk.
Bonnie and Nan stepped from behind the door.
George and Bill were hiding on the bookcase.

"Happy birthday!" said Jill, giving Gwen a hug.

For once Gwen didn't know what to say.

"Were you surprised?" asked Risa.

Gwen wiped a tear from her eye. She was so surprised, she could hardly talk.

"Wait a minute," said Gwen. "You mean the picture was never stolen. Where is it?"

"It's right here," said Jill, pointing to her wall. "I wanted a mystery to surprise you."

"The long blond hair was mine," said Tanya. "I sacrificed some of it for your birthday."

(THE PAINTING OF JILL AND FLETCHER) →

TANYA

Gwen giggled. "I should have guessed," said Gwen. Tanya had the prettiest hair of all their friends.

"We had to keep quiet in the dark for so, so long," said Risa. "It was scary."

They went into the dining room. Gwen sat down at the head of the table and put on her party hat. "Sit next to me," Gwen whispered to Jill. Jill grinned from ear to ear. "This was so much fun to plan."

They had hot dogs and French fries and lemonade, all of Gwen's favorites. Gwen thought it was her best birthday ever.

"It's time for the presents and the cake," said Jill. "It's a cake to end all cakes—so big, we couldn't hide it in the kitchen. I had to put it in the closet with your presents."

Jill went to the big hall closet. She let out a scream. "Everything's missing, even the cake."

Gwen and the others rushed to Jill's side.

"The presents!" cried Risa. "All the presents are missing!"

Gwen doubled over laughing. Jill stared at her. "What's so funny?" Gwen slapped Jill on the back. "You are too much." Gwen was laughing so hard she was practically snorting.

"This isn't a joke," said Jill. "All your presents are missing."

"You can fool me once, but you can't do it twice," said Gwen. "This is another mystery game for my birthday."

Gwen got down on all fours and searched the floor of the closet. "Maybe this is a clue," joked Gwen, pulling out an empty shopping bag from the bookstore in the mall.

"Here's another shopping bag from The Toy Barn," said Ona. "You must have gotten some pretty neat presents."

"Here's one from Ferguson's department store," said Isa.

They found lots of empty shopping bags, but no presents.

Gwen studied all the shopping bags. She tapped her braces. "It's a treasure hunt!" she exclaimed. "I'm supposed to follow the clues to the mall. This is fun. Let's go."

Jill's mother came out with a big mound of ice cream. "I thought it was time for the cake and to open the presents," she said.

"There's no cake and no presents," groaned Jill.

"I don't understand," said Jill's mom. "I saw them come in. I put them in the closet myself."

"Don't ask," said Jill to her mother. "At least Gwen's having a good time."

TAP TAP TAP TAP TAP TAP TAP

The whole party trooped to the mall. Gwen showed the shopping bag to the bookstore owner. "It's my birthday," said Gwen proudly. "And we're playing one of those mystery games. I think your shopping bag is a clue. Can you help us?"

Jill looked embarrassed.

The bookstore owner took her shopping bag.
"It's got frosting on it," she said. She looked down
at Willie. "You bought some mysteries the other
day, didn't you?" she said.

Willie put his finger to his lips and pointed to
Gwen. "It's her birthday," he mouthed.

Gwen looked at him suspiciously.

At The Toy Barn the salesclerk recognized
Risa. "You bought the Singing Rocking Dragon."

Risa blushed. "I didn't want Gwen to know,"
she whispered.

"I love Rocking Dragons," said Gwen. "I
always wanted one."

"But . . . it's been stolen," wailed Risa.

Finally, after going to a lot of stores, Gwen
was stumped. "This mystery game is too hard for
me," she admitted. "Let's go back to Jill's house,"
she said. "This has been fun, but now I want to
open my presents." Jill didn't know what to say.

Fletcher was waiting for them on the front steps. His lips were lined with chocolate frosting. Gwen put her arm around Jill's shoulder. "Okay, pal. Let's have my cake and I'll open my presents."

"Read my lips," said Jill. "There is no cake. There are no presents. They've been stolen."

"This isn't a joke?" asked Gwen.

"The missing picture was a game," said Jill, "but this isn't."

Gwen sat down in shock next to Fletcher. "*All* my presents gone!" she groaned. "All I have are the shopping bags?"

Gwen's friends gathered around her. "Your surprise cake was very special," Jill added.

Gwen looked so sad that Fletcher licked her face. Gwen hugged him back.

"Chocolate!" Gwen exclaimed. "Fletcher's been eating chocolate. Maybe it really is a clue."

"Your special cake had chocolate all over it," said Jill excitedly. "I put it in the closet with your presents. I had my reasons. If we ever find it, I still want to surprise you."

Gwen tapped her braces. She looked at all her friends. "I think I know who stole my presents," she said quietly.

GWEN ↥   FLETCHER ↥   JILL ↥

"Who?" asked Jill.

"I'm not telling," said Gwen. "I don't know where my presents are, but one of you does."

All the kids at the birthday party looked at one another uneasily.

"Is this still a game?" asked Risa.

Gwen shook her head. She walked in circles, tapping her braces. Fletcher followed her. Then he lay down. Fletcher had eaten so much chocolate frosting, he could hardly move.

(CHOCOLATE PAW PRINTS)

Gwen stared down at his paw prints. Each one left traces of chocolate. There were paw prints leading to the backyard.

"Fletcher's doghouse!" exclaimed Gwen. "I bet those paw prints lead right to my presents."

The whole party raced to Fletcher's doghouse.
Inside the doghouse, all Gwen's presents were
piled high in the back.

"Hooray for Gwen!" shouted Willie. "She solved her own mystery."

"Help me get them back to the house," said Gwen.

Everyone grabbed a present and started for the house. Gwen took Sam's arm. "Not so fast," she whispered. "I want to talk to you and Jill."

Sam put down the present. "What do you want?" he asked.

"Why did you steal all my presents?" asked Gwen. "There were shopping bags for presents from everybody except you and Jill. It couldn't have been Jill. So it had to be you."

"It could so have been Jill," said Sam. "Why me?"

" 'Cause my present wasn't bought at a store," said Jill. "I had my cousin paint a picture of Fletcher, Gwen, and me. There was no shopping bag."

"I knew it wasn't you, anyhow," whispered Gwen.

Sam started to run. "Wait a minute, Sam,"
cried Gwen. "I just want to . . ."
Sam pushed her out of the way.

He ran back through the house, tripping on balloons and streamers.

He was almost out the front door when he tripped on Fletcher, who was lying on the front steps again.

"What's going on?" asked all the kids from the party.

"Something queer at the birthday party," said Gwen, sitting on Sam. "We'll be there in a minute."

Jill stared down at Sam. "Why did you do it?" Jill demanded. "You almost ruined Gwen's surprise."

Sam looked near tears himself. "Do you know what it's like to have a birthday the day after Christmas?" he wailed. "I never get many presents. I never had a surprise party. I was just so jealous, I had to do something."

CLOSE-UP OF SAM POCKETING SOME OF THE INVITATIONS

"You didn't mail some of the invitations, did you?" accused Jill. "You're a first-class creep!"

"Wait a minute, Jill," said Gwen. She let Sam up and dusted him off. "I sort of feel sorry for Sam."

"Where's my special cake?" demanded Jill.

"In the garage," Sam said. "Fletcher got into the closet and was eating it. I saved the cake, but when I saw the presents, I couldn't control myself. I wasn't going to keep them all. I just sat in the doghouse with them and pretended they were mine."

"It's your birthday," said Jill to Gwen. "What do you want to do with him?"

"Come with me," said Gwen to Sam.

Gwen went back inside and sat at the table. She made Sam sit next to her. Suddenly all the lights went out.

The kitchen door opened, and Jill brought in the biggest cake anybody had ever seen. It was so big that it had to be wheeled in on a red wagon.

"I love my cake!" exclaimed Gwen. "Even if the frosting's a little dented."

Gwen took Sam's hand. "Because Sam's birthday is so close to Christmas and he never gets a big birthday, he's going to help me blow out the candles," said Gwen.

Gwen and Sam blew with all their might. At that moment Jill stuck a pin in a balloon. Gwen jumped as the balloon burst.

A piece of salami floated down from the
balloon and Fletcher leaped out of the cake.

Just by chance Fletcher got chocolate frosting
all over Sam.

Jill's mother brought in a real cake and they
ate it all up. Then Gwen opened all her presents.
"My very favorite is the portrait of Fletcher, me,
and Jill.

"This is absolutely the very best birthday in my whole life!" exclaimed Gwen. And she gave Jill a hug.